THIRD CLASS IN INDIAN RAILWAYS

MAHATMA GANDHI

XpressPublishing
An imprint of Notion Press

Old No. 38, New No. 6
McNichols Road, Chetpet
Chennai - 600 031

First Published by Notion Press 2020

ISBN 978-1-64828-118-1

Contents

CHAPTER ONE

THIRD CLASS IN INDIAN RAILWAYS

I have now been in India for over two years and a half after my return from South Africa. Over one quarter of that time I have passed on the Indian trains travelling third class by choice. I have travelled up north as far as Lahore, down south up to Tranquebar, and from Karachi to Calcutta. Having resorted to third class travelling, among other reasons, for the purpose of studying the conditions under which this class of passengers travel, I have naturally made as critical observations as I could. I have fairly covered the majority of railway systems during this period. Now and then I have entered into correspondence with the management of the different railways about the defects that have come under my notice. But I think that the time has come when I should invite the press and the public to join in a crusade against a grievance which has too long remained unredressed, though much of it is capable of redress without great difficulty.

On the 12th instant I booked at Bombay for Madras by the mail train and paid Rs. 13-9. It was labelled to carry 22 passengers. These could only have seating accommodation. There were no bunks in this carriage whereon passengers could lie with any degree of safety or comfort. There were two nights to be passed in this train before reaching Madras. If not more than 22 passengers found their way into my carriage before we reached Poona, it was because the bolder ones kept the others at bay. With the exception of two or three insistent passengers, all had to find their sleep being seated all the time. After reaching Raichur the pressure became unbearable. The rush of passengers could not be stayed. The fighters among us found the task almost beyond them. The guards or other railway servants came in only to push in more passengers.

A defiant Memon merchant protested against this packing of passengers like sardines. In vain did he say that this was his fifth night on the train. The guard insulted him and referred him to the management at the terminus. There were during this night as many as 35 passengers in the carriage during the greater part of it. Some lay on the floor in the midst of dirt and some had to keep standing. A free fight was, at one time, avoided only by the intervention of some of the older passengers who did not want to add to the discomfort by an exhibition of temper.

On the way passengers got for tea tannin water with filthy sugar and a whitish looking liquid mis-called milk which gave this water a muddy appearance. I can vouch for the appearance, but I cite the testimony of the passengers as to the taste.

Not during the whole of the journey was the compartment once swept or cleaned. The result was that every time you walked on the floor or rather cut your way through the passengers seated on the floor, you waded through dirt.

The closet was also not cleaned during the journey and there was no water in the water tank.

Refreshments sold to the passengers were dirty-looking, handed by dirtier hands, coming out of filthy receptacles and weighed in equally unattractive scales. These were previously sampled by millions of flies. I asked some of the passengers who went in for these dainties to give their opinion. Many of them used choice expressions as to the quality but were satisfied to state that they were helpless in the matter; they had to take things as they came.

On reaching the station I found that the ghari-wala would not take me unless I paid the fare he wanted. I mildly protested and told him I would pay him the authorised fare. I had to turn passive resister before I could be taken. I simply told him he would have to pull me out of the ghari or call the policeman.

The return journey was performed in no better manner. The carriage was packed already and but for a friend's intervention I could not have been able to secure even a seat. My admission was certainly beyond the authorised number. This compartment was constructed to carry 9 passengers but it had constantly 12 in it. At one place an important railway servant swore at a protestant, threatened to strike him and locked the door over the passengers whom he had with difficulty squeezed in. To this compartment there was a closet falsely so called. It was designed as a European closet but could hardly be used as such. There was a pipe in it but no water, and I say without fear of challenge that it was pestilentially dirty.

The compartment itself was evil looking. Dirt was lying thick upon the wood work and I do not know that it had ever seen soap or water.

The compartment had an exceptional assortment of passengers. There were three stalwart Punjabi Mahomedans, two refined Tamilians and two Mahomedan merchants who joined us later. The merchants related the bribes they had to give to procure comfort. One of the Punjabis had already travelled three nights and was weary and fatigued. But he could not stretch himself. He said he had sat the whole day at the Central Station watching passengers giving bribe to procure their tickets. Another said he had himself to pay Rs. 5 before he could get his ticket and his seat. These three men were bound for Ludhiana and had still more nights of travel in store for them.

What I have described is not exceptional but normal. I have got down at Raichur, Dhond, Sonepur, Chakradharpur, Purulia, Asansol and other junction stations and been at the 'Mosafirkhanas' attached to these stations. They are discreditable-looking places where there is no order, no cleanliness but utter confusion and horrible din and noise. Passengers have no benches or not enough to sit on. They squat on dirty floors and eat dirty food. They are permitted to throw the leavings of their food and spit where they like, sit how they like and smoke everywhere. The closets attached to these places defy description. I have not the power adequately to describe them without committing a breach of the laws of decent speech. Disinfecting powder, ashes, or disinfecting fluids are unknown. The army of flies buzzing about them warns you against their use. But a third-class traveller is dumb and helpless. He does not want to complain even though to go to these places may be to court death. I know passengers who fast while they are travelling just in order to lessen the misery of their life in the trains. At Sonepur flies having failed, wasps have come forth to warn the public and the authorities, but yet to no purpose. At the Imperial Capital a certain third class booking-office is a Black-Hole fit only to be destroyed.

Is it any wonder that plague has become endemic in India? Any other result is impossible where passengers always leave some dirt where they go and take more on leaving.

On Indian trains alone passengers smoke with impunity in all carriages irrespective of the presence of the fair sex and irrespective of the protest of non-smokers. And this, notwithstanding a bye-law which prevents a passenger from smoking without the permission of his fellows in the compartment which is not allotted to smokers.

The existence of the awful war cannot be allowed to stand in the way of the removal of this gigantic evil. War can be no warrant for tolerating dirt and overcrowding. One could understand an entire stoppage of passenger traffic in a crisis like this, but never a continuation or accentuation of insanitation and conditions that must undermine health and morality.

Compare the lot of the first class passengers with that of the third class. In the Madras case the first class fare is over five times as much as the third class fare. Does the third class passenger get one-fifth, even one-tenth, of the comforts of his first class fellow? It is but simple justice to claim that some relative proportion be observed between the cost and comfort.

It is a known fact that the third class traffic pays for the ever-increasing luxuries of first and second class travelling. Surely a third class passenger is entitled at least to the bare necessities of life.

In neglecting the third class passengers, opportunity of giving a splendid education to millions in orderliness, sanitation, decent composite life and cultivation of simple and clean tastes is being lost. Instead of receiving an object lesson in these matters third class passengers have their sense of decency and cleanliness blunted during their travelling experience.

Among the many suggestions that can be made for dealing with the evil here described, I would respectfully include this: let the people in high places, the Viceroy, the Commander-in-Chief, the Rajas, Maharajas, the Imperial Councillors and others, who generally travel in superior classes, without previous warning, go through the experiences now and then of third class travelling. We would then soon see a remarkable change in the conditions of third class travelling and the uncomplaining millions will get some return for the fares they pay under the expectation of being carried from place to place with ordinary creature comforts.

FOOTNOTE:

Ranchi, September 25, 1917.

CHAPTER TWO

VERNACULARS AS MEDIA OF INSTRUCTION

It is to be hoped that Dr. Mehta's labour of love will receive the serious attention of English-educated India. The following pages were written by him for the Vedanta Kesari of Madras and are now printed in their present form for circulation throughout India. The question of vernaculars as media of instruction is of national importance; neglect of the vernaculars means national suicide. One hears many protagonists of the English language being continued as the medium of instruction pointing to the fact that English-educated Indians are the sole custodians of public and patriotic work. It would be monstrous if it were not so. For the only education given in this country is through the English language. The fact, however, is that the results are not all proportionate to the time we give to our education. We have not reacted on the masses. But I must not anticipate Dr. Mehta. He is in earnest. He writes feelingly. He has examined the pros and cons and collected a mass of evidence in support of his arguments. The latest pronouncement on the subject is that of the Viceroy. Whilst His Excellency is unable to offer a solution, he is keenly alive to the necessity of imparting instruction in our schools through the vernaculars. The Jews of Middle and Eastern Europe, who are scattered in all parts of the world, finding it necessary to have a common tongue for mutual intercourse, have raised Yiddish to the status of a language, and have succeeded in translating into Yiddish the best books to be found in the world's literature. Even they could not satisfy the soul's yearning through the many foreign tongues of which they are masters; nor did the learned few among them wish to tax the masses of the Jewish population with having to learn a foreign language before they could realise their dignity. So they have enriched what was at one time looked upon as a mere jargon—but what the Jewish children learnt from their mothers—by taking special pains to translate into it the best thought of the world. This is a truly marvellous work. It has been done during the present generation, and Webster's Dictionary defines it as a polyglot jargon used for inter-communication by Jews from different nations.

But a Jew of Middle and Eastern Europe would feel insulted if his mother tongue were now so described. If these Jewish scholars have succeeded, within a generation, in giving their masses a language of which they may feel proud, surely it should be an easy task for us to supply the needs of our own vernaculars which are cultured languages. South Africa teaches us the same lesson. There was a duel there between the Taal, a corrupt form of Dutch, and English. The Boer mothers and the Boer fathers were determined that they would not let their children, with whom they in their infancy talked in the Taal, be weighed down with having to receive instruction through English. The case for English here was a strong one. It had able pleaders for it. But English had to yield before Boer patriotism. It may be observed that they rejected even the High Dutch. The school masters, therefore, who are accustomed to speak the published Dutch of Europe, are compelled to teach the easier Taal. And literature of an excellent character is at the present moment growing up in South Africa in the Taal, which was only a few years ago, the common medium of speech between simple but brave rustics. If we have lost faith in our vernaculars, it is a sign of want of faith in ourselves; it is the surest sign of decay. And no scheme of self-government, however benevolently or generously it may be bestowed upon us, will ever make us a self-governing nation, if we have no respect for the languages our mothers speak.

FOOTNOTE:

Introduction to Dr. Mehta's "Self-Government Series".

CHAPTER THREE

SWADESHI

It was not without great diffidence that I undertook to speak to you at all. And I was hard put to it in the selection of my subject. I have chosen a very delicate and difficult subject. It is delicate because of the peculiar views I hold upon Swadeshi, and it is difficult because I have not that command of language which is necessary for giving adequate expression to my thoughts. I know that I may rely upon your indulgence for the many shortcomings you will no doubt find in my address, the more so when I tell you that there is nothing in what I am about to say that I am not either already practising or am not preparing to practise to the best of my ability. It encourages me to observe that last month you devoted a week to prayer in the place of an address. I have earnestly prayed that what I am about to say may bear fruit and I know that you will bless my word with a similar prayer.

After much thinking I have arrived at a definition of Swadeshi that, perhaps, best illustrates my meaning. Swadeshi is that spirit in us which restricts us to the use and service of our immediate surroundings to the exclusion of the more remote. Thus, as for religion, in order to satisfy the requirements of the definition, I must restrict myself to my ancestral religion. That is the use of my immediate religious surrounding. If I find it defective, I should serve it by purging it of its defects. In the domain of politics I should make use of the indigenous institutions and serve them by curing them of their proved defects. In that of economics I should use only things that are produced by my immediate neighbours and serve those industries by making them efficient and complete where they might be found wanting. It is suggested that such Swadeshi, if reduced to practice, will lead to the millennium. And, as we do not abandon our pursuit after the millennium, because we do not expect quite to reach it within our times, so may we not abandon Swadeshi even though it may not be fully attained for generations to come.

Let us briefly examine the three branches of Swadeshi as sketched above. Hinduism has become a conservative religion and, therefore, a mighty force because of the Swadeshi spirit underlying it. It is the most tolerant because it is non-proselytising, and it is as capable of expansion today as it has been found to be in the past. It has succeeded not in driving out, as I think it has been erroneously held, but in absorbing Buddhism. By reason of the Swadeshi spirit, a Hindu refuses to change his religion, not necessarily because he considers it to be the best, but because he knows that he can complement it by introducing reforms. And what I have said about Hinduism is, I suppose, true of the other great faiths of the world, only it is held that it is specially so in the case of Hinduism. But here comes the point I am labouring to reach. If there is any substance in what I have said, will not the great missionary bodies of India, to whom she owes a deep debt of gratitude for what they have done and are doing, do still better and serve the spirit of Christianity better by dropping the goal of proselytising while continuing their philanthropic work?

I hope you will not consider this to be an impertinence on my part. I make the suggestion in all sincerity and with due humility. Moreover I have some claim upon your attention. I have endeavoured to study the Bible. I consider it as part of my scriptures. The spirit of the Sermon on the Mount competes almost on equal terms with the Bhagavad Gita for the domination of my heart. I yield to no Christian in the strength of devotion with which I sing "Lead kindly light" and several other inspired hymns of a similar nature. I have come under the influence of noted Christian missionaries belonging to different denominations. And enjoy to this day the privilege of friendship with some of them. You will perhaps, therefore, allow that I have offered the above suggestion not as a biased Hindu, but as a humble and impartial student of religion with great leanings towards Christianity. May it not be that "Go ye unto all the world" message has been somewhat narrowly interpreted and the spirit of it missed? It will not be denied, I speak from experience, that many of the conversions are only so-called. In some cases the appeal has gone not to the heart but to the stomach. And in every case a conversion leaves a sore behind it which, I venture to think, is avoidable. Quoting again from experience, a new birth, a change of heart, is perfectly possible in every one of the great faiths. I know I am now treading upon thin ice. But I do not apologise in closing this part of my subject, for saying that the frightful outrage that is just going on in Europe, perhaps shows that the message of Jesus of Nazareth, the Son of Peace, had been little understood in Europe, and that light upon it may have to be thrown from the East.

I have sought your help in religious matters, which it is yours to give in a special sense. But I make bold to seek it even in political matters. I do not believe that religion has nothing to do with politics. The latter divorced from religion is like a corpse only fit to be buried. As a matter of fact, in your own silent manner, you influence politics not a little. And I feel that, if the attempt to separate politics from religion had not been made as it is even now made, they would not have degenerated as they often appear to have done. No one considers that the political life of the country is in a happy state. Following out the Swadeshi spirit, I observe the indigenous institutions and the village panchayats hold me. India is really a republican country, and it is because it is that, that it has survived every shock hitherto delivered. Princes and potentates, whether they were Indian born or foreigners, have hardly touched the vast masses except for collecting revenue. The latter in their turn seem to have rendered unto Caesar what was Caesar's and for the rest have done much as they have liked. The vast organisation of caste answered not only the religious wants of the community, but it answered to its political needs. The villagers managed their internal affairs through the caste system, and through it they dealt with any oppression from the ruling power or powers. It is not possible to deny of a nation that was capable of producing the caste system its wonderful power of organisation. One had but to attend the great Kumbha Mela at Hardwar last year to know how skilful that organisation must have been, which without any seeming effort was able effectively to cater for more than a million pilgrims. Yet it is the fashion to say that we lack organising ability. This is true, I fear, to a certain extent, of those who have been nurtured in the new traditions. We have laboured under a terrible handicap owing to an almost fatal departure from the Swadeshi spirit. We, the educated classes, have received our education through a foreign tongue. We have therefore not reacted upon the masses. We want to represent the masses, but we fail. They recognise us not much more than they recognise the English officers. Their hearts are an open book to neither. Their aspirations are not ours. Hence there is a break. And you witness not in reality failure to organise but want of correspondence between the representatives and the represented. If during the last fifty years we had been educated through the vernaculars, our elders and our servants and our neighbours would have partaken of our knowledge; the discoveries of a Bose or a Ray would have been household treasures as are the Ramayan and the Mahabharat. As it is, so far as the masses are concerned, those great discoveries might as well have been made by foreigners. Had instruction in all the branches of learning been given through the vernaculars, I make bold to say that they would have been enriched wonderfully. The question of village sanitation, etc., would have been solved long ago. The village panchayats would be now a living force in a special way, and India would almost be enjoying self-government suited to its requirements and would have been spared the humiliating spectacle of organised assassination on its sacred soil. It is not too late to mend. And you can help if you will, as no other body or bodies can.

And now for the last division of Swadeshi, much of the deep poverty of the masses is due to the ruinous departure from Swadeshi in the economic and industrial life. If not an article of commerce had been brought from outside India, she would be today a land flowing with milk and honey. But that was not to be. We were greedy and so was England. The connection between England and India was based clearly upon an error. But she does not remain in India in error. It is her declared policy that India is to be held in trust for her people. If this be true, Lancashire must stand aside. And if the Swadeshi doctrine is a sound doctrine, Lancashire can stand aside without hurt, though it may sustain a shock for the time being. I think of Swadeshi not as a boycott movement undertaken by way of revenge. I conceive it as religious principle to be followed by all. I am no economist, but I have read some treatises which show that England could easily become a self-sustained country, growing all the produce she needs. This may be an utterly ridiculous proposition, and perhaps the best proof that it cannot be true, is that England is one of the largest importers in the world. But India cannot live for Lancashire or any other country before she is able to live for herself. And she can live for herself only if she produces and is helped to produce everything for her requirements within her own borders. She need not be, she ought not to be, drawn into the vertex of mad and ruinous competition which breeds fratricide, jealousy and many other evils. But who is to stop her great millionaires from entering into the world competition? Certainly not legislation. Force of public opinion, proper education, however, can do a great deal in the desired direction. The hand-loom industry is in a dying condition. I took special care during my wanderings last year to see as many weavers as possible, and my heart ached to find how they had lost, how families had retired from this once flourishing and honourable occupation. If we follow the Swadeshi doctrine, it would be your duty and mine to find out neighbours who can supply our wants and to teach them to supply them where they do not know how to proceed, assuming that there are neighbours who are in want of healthy occupation. Then every village of India will almost be a self-supporting and self-contained unit, exchanging only such necessary commodities with other villages where they are not locally producible. This may all sound nonsensical. Well, India is a country of nonsense. It is nonsensical to parch one's throat with thirst when a kindly Mahomedan is ready to offer pure water to drink. And yet thousands of Hindus would rather die of thirst than drink water from a Mahomedan household. These nonsensical men can also, once they are convinced that their religion demands that they should wear garments manufactured in India only and eat food only grown in India, decline to wear any other clothing or eat any other food. Lord Curzon set the fashion for tea-drinking. And that pernicious drug now bids fair to overwhelm the nation. It has already undermined the digestive apparatus of hundreds of thousands of men and women and constitutes an additional tax upon their slender purses. Lord Hardinge can set the fashion for Swadeshi, and almost the whole of India forswear foreign goods. There is a verse in the Bhagavad Gita, which, freely rendered, means, masses follow the classes. It is easy to undo the evil if the thinking portion of the community were to take the Swadeshi vow even though it may, for a time, cause considerable inconvenience. I hate legislative interference, in any department of life. At best it is the lesser evil. But I would tolerate, welcome, indeed, plead for a stiff protective duty upon foreign goods. Natal, a British colony, protected its sugar by taxing the sugar that came from another British colony, Mauritius. England has sinned against India by forcing free trade upon her. It may have been food for her, but it has been poison for this country.

It has often been urged that India cannot adopt Swadeshi in the economic life at any rate. Those who advance this objection do not look upon Swadeshi as a rule of life. With them it is a mere patriotic effort not to be made if it involved any self-denial. Swadeshi, as defined here, is a religious discipline to be undergone in utter disregard of the physical discomfort it may cause to individuals. Under its spell the deprivation of a pin or a needle, because these are not manufactured in India, need cause no terror. A Swadeshist will learn to do without hundreds of things which today he considers necessary. Moreover, those who dismiss Swadeshi from their minds by arguing the impossible, forget that Swadeshi, after all, is a goal to be reached by steady effort. And we would be making for the goal even if we confined Swadeshi to a given set of articles allowing ourselves as a temporary measure to use such things as might not be procurable in the country.

There now remains for me to consider one more objection that has been raised against Swadeshi. The objectors consider it to be a most selfish doctrine without any warrant in the civilised code of morality. With them to practise Swadeshi is to revert to barbarism. I cannot enter into a detailed analysis of the position. But I would urge that Swadeshi is the only doctrine consistent with the law of humility and love. It is arrogance to think of launching out to serve the whole of India when I am hardly able to serve even my own family. It were better to concentrate my effort upon the family and consider that through them I was serving the whole nation and, if you will, the whole of humanity. This is humility and it is love. The motive will determine the quality of the act. I may serve my family regardless of the sufferings I may cause to others. As for instance, I may accept an employment which enables me to extort money from people, I enrich myself thereby and then satisfy many unlawful demands of the family. Here I am neither serving the family nor the State. Or I may recognise that God has given me hands and feet only to work with for my sustenance and for that of those who may be dependent upon me. I would then at once simplify my life and that of those whom I can directly reach. In this instance I would have served the family without causing injury to anyone else. Supposing that everyone followed this mode of life, we should have at once an ideal state. All will not reach that state at the same time. But those of us who, realising its truth, enforce it in practice will clearly anticipate and accelerate the coming of that happy day. Under this plan of life, in seeming to serve India to the exclusion of every other country I do not harm any other country. My patriotism is both exclusive and inclusive. It is exclusive in the sense that in all humility I confine my attention to the land of my birth, but it is inclusive in the sense that my service is not of a competitive or antagonistic nature. Sic utere tuo ut alienum non la is not merely a legal maxim, but it is a grand doctrine of life. It is the key to a proper practice of Ahimsa or love. It is for you, the custodians of a great faith, to set the fashion and show, by your preaching, sanctified by practice, that patriotism based on hatred "killeth" and that patriotism based on love "giveth life."

FOOTNOTE:

Address delivered before the Missionary Conference on February 14, 1916.

CHAPTER FOUR

AHIMSA

There seems to be no historical warrant for the belief that an exaggerated practice of Ahimsa synchronises with our becoming bereft of manly virtues. During the past 1,500 years we have, as a nation, given ample proof of physical courage, but we have been torn by internal dissensions and have been dominated by love of self instead of love of country. We have, that is to say, been swayed by the spirit of irreligion rather than of religion.

I do not know how far the charge of unmanliness can be made good against the Jains. I hold no brief for them. By birth I am a Vaishnavite, and was taught Ahimsa in my childhood. I have derived much religious benefit from Jain religious works as I have from scriptures of the other great faiths of the world. I owe much to the living company of the deceased philosopher, Rajachand Kavi, who was a Jain by birth. Thus, though my views on Ahimsa are a result of my study of most of the faiths of the world, they are now no longer dependent upon the authority of these works. They are a part of my life, and, if I suddenly discovered that the religious books read by me bore a different interpretation from the one I had learnt to give them, I should still hold to the view of Ahimsa as I am about to set forth here.

Our Shastras seem to teach that a man who really practises Ahimsa in its fulness has the world at his feet; he so affects his surroundings that even the snakes and other venomous reptiles do him no harm. This is said to have been the experience of St. Francis of Assisi.

In its negative form it means not injuring any living being whether by body or mind. It may not, therefore, hurt the person of any wrong-doer, or bear any ill-will to him and so cause him mental suffering. This statement does not cover suffering caused to the wrong-doer by natural acts of mine which do not proceed from ill-will. It, therefore, does not prevent me from withdrawing from his presence a child whom he, we shall imagine, is about to strike. Indeed, the proper practice of Ahimsa requires me to withdraw the intended victim from the wrong-doer, if I am, in any way whatsoever, the guardian of such a child. It was, therefore, most proper for the passive resisters of South Africa to have resisted the evil that the Union Government sought to do to them. They bore no ill-will to it. They showed this by helping the Government whenever it needed their help. Their resistance consisted of disobedience of the orders of the Government, even to the extent of suffering death at their hands. Ahimsa requires deliberate self-suffering, not a deliberate injuring of the supposed wrong-doer.

In its positive form, Ahimsa means the largest love, the greatest charity. If I am a follower of Ahimsa, I must love my enemy. I must apply the same rules to the wrong-doer who is my enemy or a stranger to me, as I would to my wrong-doing father or son. This active Ahimsa necessarily includes truth and fearlessness. As man cannot deceive the loved one, he does not fear or frighten him or her. Gift of life is the greatest of all gifts; a man who gives it in reality, disarms all hostility. He has paved the way for an honourable understanding. And none who is himself subject to fear can bestow that gift. He must, therefore, be himself fearless. A man cannot then practice Ahimsa and be a coward at the same time. The practice of Ahimsa calls forth the greatest courage. It is the most soldierly of a soldier's virtues. General Gordon has been represented in a famous statue as bearing only a stick. This takes us far on the road to Ahimsa. But a soldier, who needs the protection of even a stick, is to that extent so much the less a soldier. He is the true soldier who knows how to die and stand his ground in the midst of a hail of bullets. Such a one was Ambarisha, who stood his ground without lifting a finger though Duryasa did his worst. The Moors who were being pounded by the French gunners and who rushed to the guns' mouths with 'Allah' on their lips, showed much the same type of courage. Only theirs was the courage of desperation. Ambarisha's was due to love. Yet the Moorish valour, readiness to die, conquered the gunners. They frantically waved their hats, ceased firing, and greeted their erstwhile enemies as comrades. And so the South African passive resisters in their thousands were ready to die rather than sell their honour for a little personal ease. This was Ahimsa in its active form. It never barters away honour. A helpless girl in the hands of a follower of Ahimsa finds better and surer protection than in the hands of one who is prepared to defend her only to the point to which his weapons would carry him. The tyrant, in the first instance, will have to walk to his victim over the dead body of her defender; in the second, he has but to overpower the defender; for it is assumed that the cannon of propriety in the second instance will be satisfied when the defender has fought to the extent of his physical valour. In the first instance, as the defender has matched his very soul against the mere body of the tyrant, the odds are that the soul in the latter will be awakened, and the girl would stand an infinitely greater chance of her honour being protected than in any other conceivable circumstance, barring of course, that of her own personal courage.

If we are unmanly today, we are so, not because we do not know how to strike, but because we fear to die. He is no follower of Mahavira, the apostle of Jainism, or of Buddha or of the Vedas, who being afraid to die, takes flight before any danger, real or imaginary, all the while wishing that somebody else would remove the danger by destroying the person causing it. He is no follower of Ahimsa who does not care a straw if he kills a man by inches by deceiving him in trade, or who would protect by force of arms a few cows and make away with the butcher or who, in order to do a supposed good to his country, does not mind killing off a few officials. All these are actuated by hatred, cowardice and fear. Here the love of the cow or the country is a vague thing intended to satisfy one's vanity, or soothe a stinging conscience.

Ahimsa truly understood is in my humble opinion a panacea for all evils mundane and extra-mundane. We can never overdo it. Just at present we are not doing it at all. Ahimsa does not displace the practice of other virtues, but renders their practice imperatively necessary before it can be practised even in its rudiments. Mahavira and Buddha were soldiers, and so was Tolstoy. Only they saw deeper and truer into their profession, and found the secret of a true, happy, honourable and godly life. Let us be joint sharers with these teachers, and this land of ours will once more be the abode of gods.

FOOTNOTE:

The Modern Review, October, 1916.

CHAPTER FIVE

THE MORAL BASIS OF CO-OPERATION

The only claim I have on your indulgence is that some months ago I attended with Mr. Ewbank a meeting of mill-hands to whom he wanted to explain the principles of co-operation. The chawl in which they were living was as filthy as it well could be. Recent rains had made matters worse. And I must frankly confess that, had it not been for Mr. Ewbank's great zeal for the cause he has made his own, I should have shirked the task. But there we were, seated on a fairly worn-out charpai, surrounded by men, women and children. Mr. Ewbank opened fire on a man who had put himself forward and who wore not a particularly innocent countenance. After he had engaged him and the other people about him in Gujrati conversation, he wanted me to speak to the people. Owing to the suspicious looks of the man who was first spoken to, I naturally pressed home the moralities of co-operation. I fancy that Mr. Ewbank rather liked the manner in which I handled the subject. Hence, I believe, his kind invitation to me to tax your patience for a few moments upon a consideration of co-operation from a moral standpoint.

My knowledge of the technicality of co-operation is next to nothing. My brother, Devadhar, has made the subject his own. Whatever he does, naturally attracts me and predisposes me to think that there must be something good in it and the handling of it must be fairly difficult. Mr. Ewbank very kindly placed at my disposal some literature too on the subject. And I have had a unique opportunity of watching the effect of some co-operative effort in Champaran. I have gone through Mr. Ewbank's ten main points which are like the Commandments, and I have gone through the twelve points of Mr. Collins of Behar, which remind me of the law of the Twelve Tables. There are so-called agricultural banks in Champaran. They were to me disappointing efforts, if they were meant to be demonstrations of the success of co-operation. On the other hand, there is quiet work in the same direction being done by Mr. Hodge, a missionary whose efforts are leaving their impress on those who come in contact with him. Mr. Hodge is a co-operative enthusiast and probably considers that the result which he sees flowing from his efforts are due to the working of co-operation. I, who was able to watch the efforts, had no hesitation in inferring that the personal equation counted for success in the one and failure in the other instance.

I am an enthusiast myself, but twenty-five years of experimenting and experience have made me a cautious and discriminating enthusiast. Workers in a cause necessarily, though quite unconsciously, exaggerate its merits and often succeed in turning its very defects into advantages. In spite of my caution I consider the little institution I am conducting in Ahmedabad as the finest thing in the world. It alone gives me sufficient inspiration. Critics tell me that it represents a soulless soul-force and that its severe discipline has made it merely mechanical. I suppose both—the critics and I—are wrong. It is, at best, a humble attempt to place at the disposal of the nation a home where men and women may have scope for free and unfettered development of character, in keeping with the national genius, and, if its controllers do not take care, the discipline that is the foundation of character may frustrate the very end in view. I would venture, therefore, to warn enthusiasts in co-operation against entertaining false hopes.

With Sir Daniel Hamilton it has become a religion. On the 13th January last, he addressed the students of the Scottish Churches College and, in order to point a moral, he instanced Scotland's poverty of two hundred years ago and showed how that great country was raised from a condition of poverty to plenty. "There were two powers, which raised her—the Scottish Church and the Scottish banks. The Church manufactured the men and the banks manufactured the money to give the men a start in life.... The Church disciplined the nation in the fear of God which is the beginning of wisdom and in the parish schools of the Church the children learned that the chief end of man's life was to glorify God and to enjoy Him for ever. Men were trained to believe in God and in themselves, and on the trustworthy character so created the Scottish banking system was built." Sir Daniel then shows that it was possible to build up the marvellous Scottish banking system only on the character so built. So far there can only be perfect agreement with Sir Daniel, for that 'without character there is no co-operation' is a sound maxim. But he would have us go much further. He thus waxes eloquent on co-operation: "Whatever may be your daydreams of India's future, never forget this that it is to weld India into one, and so enable her to take her rightful place in the world, that the British Government is here; and the welding hammer in the hand of the Government is the co-operative movement." In his opinion it is the panacea of all the evils that afflict India at the present moment. In its extended sense it can justify the claim on one condition which need not be mentioned here; in the limited sense in which Sir Daniel has used it, I venture to think, it is an enthusiast's exaggeration. Mark his peroration: "Credit, which is only Trust and Faith, is becoming more and more the money power of the world, and in the parchment bullet into which is impressed the faith which removes mountains, India will find victory and peace." Here there is evident confusion of thought. The credit which is becoming the money power of the world has little moral basis and is not a synonym for Trust or Faith, which are purely moral qualities. After twenty years' experience of hundreds of men, who had dealings with banks in South Africa, the opinion I had so often heard expressed has become firmly rooted in me, that the greater the rascal the greater the credit he enjoys with his banks. The banks do not pry into his moral character: they are satisfied that he meets his overdrafts and promissory notes punctually. The credit system has encircled this beautiful globe of ours like a serpent's coil, and if we do not mind, it bids fair to crush us out of breath. I have witnessed the ruin of many a home through the system, and it has made no difference whether the credit was labelled co-operative or otherwise. The deadly coil has made possible the devastating spectacle in Europe, which we are helplessly looking on. It was perhaps never so true as it is today that, as in law so in war, the longest purse finally wins. I have ventured to give prominence to the current belief about credit system in order to emphasise the point that the co-operative movement will be a blessing to India only to the extent that it is a moral movement strictly directed by men fired with religious fervour. It follows, therefore, that co-operation should be confined to men wishing to be morally right, but failing to do so, because of grinding poverty or of the grip of the Mahajan. Facility for obtaining loans at fair rates will not make immoral men moral. But the wisdom of the Estate or philanthropists demands that they should help on the onward path, men struggling to be good.

Too often do we believe that material prosperity means moral growth. It is necessary that a movement which is fraught with so much good to India should not degenerate into one for merely advancing cheap loans. I was therefore delighted to read the recommendation in the Report of the Committee on Co-operation in India, that "they wish clearly to express their opinion that it is to true co-operation alone, that is, to a co-operation which recognises the moral aspect of the question that Government must look for the amelioration of the masses and not to a pseudo-co-operative edifice, however imposing, which is built in ignorance of co-operative principles." With this standard before us, we will not measure the success of the movement by the number of co-operative societies formed, but by the moral condition of the co-operators. The registrars will, in that event, ensure the moral growth of existing societies before multiplying them. And the Government will make their promotion conditional, not upon the number of societies they have registered, but the moral success of the existing institutions. This will mean tracing the course of every pie lent to the members. Those responsible for the proper conduct of co-operative societies will see to it that the money advanced does not find its way into the toddy-seller's bill or into the pockets of the keepers of gambling dens. I would excuse the rapacity of the Mahajan if it has succeeded in keeping the gambling die or toddy from the ryot's home.

A word perhaps about the Mahajan will not be out of place. Co-operation is not a new device. The ryots co-operate to drum out monkeys or birds that destroy their crops. They co-operate to use a common thrashing floor. I have found them co-operate to protect their cattle to the extent of their devoting the best land for the grazing of their cattle. And they have been found co-operating against a particular rapacious Mahajan. Doubts have been expressed as to the success of co-operation because of the tightness of the Mahajan's hold on the ryots. I do not share the fears. The mightiest Mahajan must, if he represent an evil force, bend before co-operation, conceived as an essentially moral movement. But my limited experience of the Mahajan of Champaran has made me revise the accepted opinion about his 'blighting influence.' I have found him to be not always relentless, not always exacting of the last pie. He sometimes serves his clients in many ways and even comes to their rescue in the hour of their distress. My observation is so limited that I dare not draw any conclusions from it, but I respectfully enquire whether it is not possible to make a serious effort to draw out the good in the Mahajan and help him or induce him to throw out the evil in him. May he not be induced to join the army of co-operation, or has experience proved that he is past praying for?

I note that the movement takes note of all indigenous industries. I beg publicly to express my gratitude to Government for helping me in my humble effort to improve the lot of the weaver. The experiment I am conducting shows that there is a vast field for work in this direction. No well-wisher of India, no patriot dare look upon the impending destruction of the hand-loom weaver with equanimity. As Dr. Mann has stated, this industry used to supply the peasant with an additional source of livelihood and an insurance against famine. Every registrar who will nurse back to life this important and graceful industry will earn the gratitude of India. My humble effort consists firstly in making researches as to the possibilities of simple reforms in the orthodox hand-looms, secondly, in weaning the educated youth from the craving for Government or other services and the feeling that education renders him unfit for independent occupation and inducing him to take to weaving as a calling as honourable as that of a barrister or a doctor, and thirdly by helping those weavers who have abandoned their occupation to revert to it. I will not weary the audience with any statement on the first two parts of the experiment. The third may be allowed a few sentences as it has a direct bearing upon the subject before us. I was able to enter upon it only six months ago. Five families that had left off the calling have reverted to it and they are doing a prosperous business. The Ashram supplies them at their door with the yarn they need; its volunteers take delivery of the cloth woven, paying them cash at the market rate. The Ashram merely loses interest on the loan advanced for the yarn. It has as yet suffered no loss and is able to restrict its loss to a minimum by limiting the loan to a particular figure. All future transactions are strictly cash. We are able to command a ready sale for the cloth received. The loss of interest, therefore, on the transaction is negligible. I would like the audience to note its purely moral character from start to finish. The Ashram depends for its existence on such help as friends render it. We, therefore, can have no warrant for charging interest. The weavers could not be saddled with it. Whole families that were breaking to pieces are put together again. The use of the loan is predetermined. And we, the middlemen, being volunteers, obtain the privilege of entering into the lives of these families, I hope, for their and our betterment. We cannot lift them without being lifted ourselves. This last relationship has not yet been developed, but we hope, at an early date, to take in hand the education too of these families and not rest satisfied till we have touched them at every point. This is not too ambitious a dream. God willing, it will be a reality some day. I have ventured to dilate upon the small experiment to illustrate what I mean by co-operation to present it to others for imitation. Let us be sure of our ideal. We shall ever fail to realise it, but we should never cease to strive for it. Then there need be no fear of "co-operation of scoundrels" that Ruskin so rightly dreaded.

FOOTNOTE

Paper contributed to the Bombay Provincial Co-operative Conference, September 17, 1917.

CHAPTER SIX

NATIONAL DRESS

I have hitherto successfully resisted to temptation of either answering your or Mr. Irwin's criticism of the humble work I am doing in Champaran. Nor am I going to succumb now except with regard to a matter which Mr. Irwin has thought fit to dwell upon and about which he has not even taken the trouble of being correctly informed. I refer to his remarks on my manner of dressing.

My "familiarity with the minor amenities of Western civilisation" has taught me to respect my national costume, and it may interest Mr. Irwin to know that the dress I wear in Champaran is the dress I have always worn in India except that for a very short period in India I fell an easy prey in common with the rest of my countrymen to the wearing of semi-European dress in the courts and elsewhere outside Kathiawar. I appeared before the Kathiawar courts now 21 years ago in precisely the dress I wear in Champaran.

One change I have made and it is that, having taken to the occupation of weaving and agriculture and having taken the vow of Swadeshi, my clothing is now entirely hand-woven and hand-sewn and made by me or my fellow workers. Mr. Irwin's letter suggests that I appear before the ryots in a dress I have temporarily and specially adopted in Champaran to produce an effect. The fact is that I wear the national dress because it is the most natural and the most becoming for an Indian. I believe that our copying of the European dress is a sign of our degradation, humiliation and our weakness, and that we are committing a national sin in discarding a dress which is best suited to the Indian climate and which, for its simplicity, art and cheapness, is not to be beaten on the face of the earth and which answers hygienic requirements. Had it not been for a false pride and equally false notions of prestige, Englishmen here would long ago have adopted the Indian costume. I may mention incidentally that I do not go about Champaran bare headed. I do avoid shoes for sacred reasons. But I find too that it is more natural and healthier to avoid them whenever possible.

I am sorry to inform Mr. Irwin and your readers that my esteemed friend Babu Brijakishore Prasad, the "ex-Hon. Member of Council," still remains unregenerate and retains the provincial cap and never walks barefoot and "kicks up" a terrible noise even in the house we are living in by wearing wooden sandals. He has still not the courage, in spite of most admirable contact with me, to discard his semi-anglicised dress and whenever he goes to see officials he puts his legs into the bifurcated garment and on his own admission tortures himself by cramping his feet in inelastic shoes. I cannot induce him to believe that his clients won't desert him and the courts won't punish him if he wore his more becoming and less expensive dhoti. I invite you and Mr. Irwin not to believe the "stories" that the latter hears about me and my friends, but to join me in the crusade against educated Indians abandoning their manners, habits and customs which are not proved to be bad or harmful. Finally I venture to warn you and Mr. Irwin that you and he will ill-serve the cause both of you consider is in danger by reason of my presence in Champaran if you continue, as you have done, to base your strictures on unproved facts. I ask you to accept my assurance that I should deem myself unworthy of the friendship and confidence of hundreds of my English friends and associates—not all of them fellow cranks—if in similar circumstances I acted towards them differently from my own countrymen.

FOOTNOTE:

Reply to Mr. Irwin's criticism of his dress in the Pioneer.

www.ingramcontent.com/pod-product-compliance
Lightning Source LLC
LaVergne TN
LVHW041301150826
845673LV00008B/2682

9781648281181